Fireman S
Deep Trouble

Photographs by John Walker

04727

Dilys is having breakfast at Bella's Café. "Ever such an interesting programme on telly, last night," she says, spilling her tea. "Apparently, we could have an earthquake near here!"

Bella is puzzled. "What kind of cake?" she asks. Dilys is not amused. "Not cake – EARTHQUAKE! A landslide – because of the old mine up in the hillside. Glad I don't live near there!"

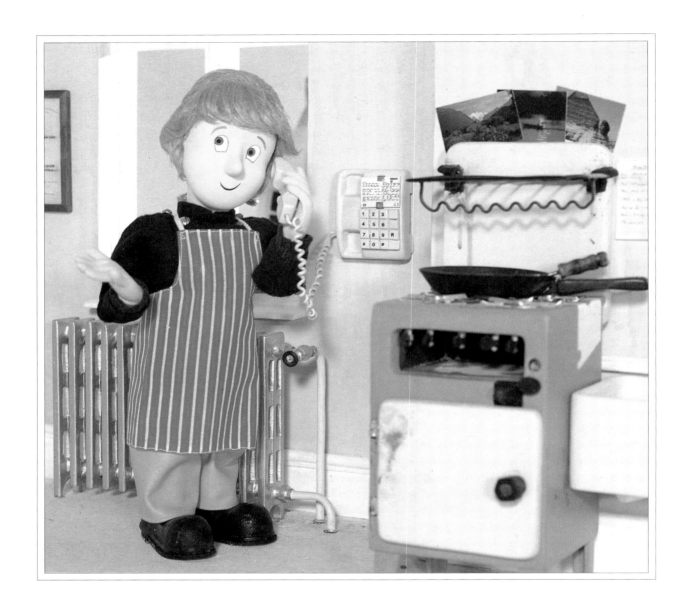

At the fire station, Penny is having her breakfast, too. "I'm fed up – it's all cooking and no firefighting!" she tells Fireman Sam on the phone. "And no time to weed my new garden."

"It's just as boring being on holiday," says Sam, "and I've only been away a day! Why don't I pop up to your new cottage and give the garden a tidy-up?" Penny is delighted.

Penny has a new home: a pretty, little cottage up on the Pontypandy hillside. It has a beautiful view over the valley, but the back garden looks on to the remains of the old mine.

Sam is working hard in the garden, digging up the earth and making new flower beds. "Now this is fun!" he thinks. "Penny won't recognise this garden when I've finished with it!"

Suddenly, there's a distant rumble. The lean-to shed shakes a little and all the pots fall off the shelves. Sam is puzzled. "It looks too sunny for a thunderstorm," he thinks.

"Was that thunder, I wonder?" thinks Trevor. He is driving James and Sarah to Penny's cottage. They have bought lots of new plants for the garden as a surprise.

Sam is still digging when the rumbling sound returns, much louder this time. The lean-to collapses, the paving stones split in two and the ground begins to shake and open!

"I'm sure I didn't dig that deeply!" thinks a worried Sam. He tries to jump to safety but it's too late. The flower bed gives way and he starts to sink – down, down, down.

Sam is stuck and up to his neck in soil. "I'm in deep trouble, here!" he thinks. Trevor and the children arrive. "Hello there," calls Sam. "Just doing a spot of digging," he jokes, bravely.

"Oh, Uncle," says Sarah, amazed. "You're supposed to plant the flowers, not yourself!" Trevor chuckles, but he knows that Sam is in danger. "I'd better dial 999," he says.

Station Officer Steele has received Trevor's call. He's on board Jupiter with Elvis and Penny at his side. "I'm glad you're driving, Penny," says Elvis. "You'll know the way!"

Penny takes a short cut and they arrive in double-quick time. "Oh, Sam," she gasps when she sees him, "you have dug yourself into a hole!" Station Officer Steele is not amused.

"Sorry, Sir," says Penny. "Permission to use the suction pipe?" she asks. "Good idea, Firefighter Morris," replies the chief. Elvis throws Sam a rope. "Hang on, Sam!" he shouts.

Elvis takes up the strain on the rope. Station Officer Steele comes to help him. "Good work Firefighter Cridlington!" he bellows. "Now we can stop him from slipping any further."

Penny gets to work with the suction pipe. "We'll soon have you out of here," she reassures Sam, and quickly hoovers up the soil. "Ready, Sir!" she calls to Station Officer Steele.

"Pull!" shouts Station Officer Steele and out pops Sam like a cork out of a bottle! There's another rumble and then the fence collapses, but Sam is safe – just in time!

Sam soon recovers. "Well done, Firefighter Morris!" says a proud Station Officer Steele. "Yes, thank you, Penny," Sam continues. "I'm sorry about the mess, it was a landslide."

"Don't worry," Penny smiles. "The Council are sending their engineers to make the cottage and garden safe again. What an exciting day it's turned out to be, after all!"

A week later Sam is still on holiday relaxing in beautiful surroundings. But he's not at an expensive hotel, he's in Penny's garden. It's completely transformed!

Penny arrives home with Trevor. "Oh, Sam it's. . .it's amazing!" she gasps. "Did you do it all yourself?" Sam smiles. "Well, Trevor did give me a hand," he admits.

"So did we!" chorus the children. "Now that the cottage is safe," continues Sam, "we thought we'd turn your landslide into a real landscape! Welcome home, Penny!"